DRAGONBREATH

BY
URSULA VERNON

SCHOLASTIC INC.
New York Toronto London Auckland
Sydney Mexico City New Delhi Hong Kong

For Deb,
for telling the right anecdote at the right time

ISBN 978-0-545-24541-8

12 11 10 9 8 7 6 5 4 3 2   11 12 13 14 15 16/0

Printed in the U.S.A.   23

First Scholastic paperback printing, September 2011

Designed by Lily Malcom
Text set in Stempel Schneidler

DRAGONBREATH

THE SEA WAS CALM...

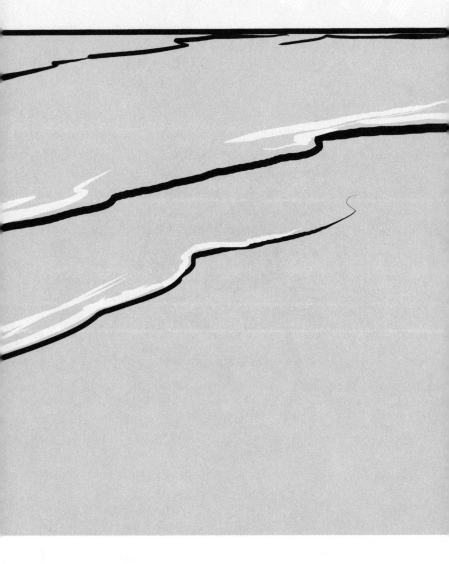

THIS WAS BETTER THAN SCHOOL. THE ONLY LOCKER FOR A HUNDRED MILES BELONGED TO DAVY JONES. HE WAS STILL THE ONLY DRAGON IN A CREW OF FROGS AND LIZARDS, BUT NOW HE WAS THE TERROR OF THE SEAS! NO ONE MADE FUN OF HIS MYTHICAL STATUS, OR HE'D MAKE THEM WALK THE PLANK!

THERE WAS JUST ONE PROBLEM . . .

WHERE WAS THAT *BEEPING* COMING FROM?

HOT THOUGHTS

Danny Dragonbreath came awake with a yelp and took a swing at his alarm clock. He missed— missed again—succeeded in knocking it onto the floor, where it beeped at him sideways—and finally had to accept that he was awake.

"Unnngggghh . . ."* he said, and groped around for the relentlessly beeping alarm clock.

 BEEP BEEP BEEP BEEP BEEP BEEP BEEP BEEP BEEP BEEP BEEP

---

* Approximate translation

Eventually he found it and turned it off, then staggered around his bedroom until he found a T-shirt. He put the shirt on backward, wondered why the tag kept poking him in the neck, and took it off again.

Mornings were not Danny's strong suit.

Finally he got the T-shirt the right way around, if inside-out, and clomped down the stairs for breakfast. He could smell bacon cooking. It smelled wonderful.

His mother was sitting at the kitchen table staring grimly into her cup of coffee. His father was cooking.

"Good morning, Danny!" said Mr. Dragonbreath, who was a morning person.

"Mrrgghhh," said Mrs. Dragonbreath, who was not.

"Morning, Dad. Err . . . morning, Mom . . ." Danny dropped into his seat at the kitchen table. The smells were making his mouth water.

Mr. Dragonbreath pulled a strip of bacon out

of the skillet, eyed it, and breathed a tiny puff of flame on it. It sizzled.

Danny watched enviously. Despite his best efforts, he still couldn't breathe fire.

As if his father could read Danny's thoughts, Mr. Dragonbreath turned around, sliding eggs and bacon onto a plate. "So, Danny! Any luck with the fire-breathing? Want to try cooking your own?"

"No, Dad," mumbled Danny. He slid down a little in his chair.

"Oh, come on . . ." His dad held out a strip of bacon. "Think hot thoughts."

Danny stood, took a deep breath, and tried to think hot thoughts, whatever that meant—deserts, firecrackers, jalapeño peppers. He exhaled vigorously, but all he got was a vague ashy taste in his mouth.

Mr. Dragonbreath frowned. "Have you been *practicing*?"

"Yes!"

His father sighed. "Eggs, dear?" he asked Mrs. Dragonbreath.

Mrs. Dragonbreath growled something, which may have included the word *no*.

"Now dear, you know that breakfast is the most important meal of the day. . . ."

Mrs. Dragonbreath looked up from her coffee, focused her eyes with some difficulty, and hissed like a cobra. (Cobras are also traditionally not morning people.)

Mr. Dragonbreath, who had been happily married to Danny's mother for a number of years, carefully poured her another cup of coffee. He did not say anything more about the most important meal of the day.

Instead he turned his attention back to Danny. Along with breakfast, Danny got a full twenty-minute pep talk on applying himself, interspersed with what were probably meant to be inspiring stories of reptiles pulling themselves up by their bootstraps and Making Something of Themselves. Mr. Dragonbreath's boss had brought in three motivational speakers in the last month to talk to all the employees at the antacid bottling plant, and Danny was suffering the fallout.

The really unfair bit was that Danny *was* applying himself, at least to breathing fire. He practiced diligently every evening. He used to practice during math class, but stopped after his math teacher called an ambulance last month. (She thought he was hyperventilating.) It was a shame, because as far as Danny was concerned, fire-breathing practice was the only thing math class was good for.

But no matter how often or where Danny practiced, he just couldn't get the knack of breathing fire. Thinking hot thoughts, visualizing his mouth as a flamethrower, gargling with kerosene twice a week—none of it did any good.

It was impossible to explain this to his father, however, who believed the key to success was more inspirational stories.

Finally he cut in—"Sorry, Dad, gotta catch the bus!"

"Oh. Right. Have a good day at school!"

His mother aimed a kiss in his general direction, then went back to her coffee.

Thank goodness for the bus, Danny thought, grabbing his backpack and running for the door.

Otherwise he would probably still have been trapped at the table, listening to another story of a dragon who had started out with nothing but two poker chips and a bent spoon and had gone on to build a hoard the size of Los Angeles.

SNORKELBATS

Danny stood at the bus stop and waited, which is what one generally does at bus stops.

Under normal circumstances he would have been restless. Danny hated standing still for anything. It was just dragonish nature. Dragons slept on their hoards, they fought knights, they occasionally flew around terrorizing peasants, but they didn't usually stand still. (It's worth noting that Danny's parents had never terrorized a peasant in their lives, and Danny's mother always volunteered to bring goodies to the school bake sale, but really, it was the principle of the thing.)

While he waited, Danny thought about the dream he'd had last night. (It certainly beat thinking about the lecture he'd gotten this morning.) It had been the most wonderful dream . . . something about a pirate ship and Captain Dragonbreath. Wendell had been in it, he definitely remembered that . . .

As if the thought had summoned him, Danny's best friend, Wendell, trudged up the sidewalk to the bus stop. Wendell was a green iguana, although he was a much more grayish green than Danny. He wore thick glasses and an expression that said he expected the worst to happen at any moment.

"Hey," said Danny.

"Hey," said Wendell.

Pleasantries concluded, they stood and waited for the bus.

"I had a dream last night that we were pirates," said Danny.

"Pirates?" Wendell shoved his glasses up his snout. "What kind of pirates?"

"I dunno," said Danny, "the usual kind, I guess . . ."

Wendell rolled his eyes. "Privateers? Rumrunners? Smugglers?"

Danny sighed. Wendell sometimes had a tendency to overthink things. "*Pirate* pirates. You know. Yo ho, avast me hearties, all that . . ."

"What does *avast* mean, anyway? I've always wondered."

"Hey, look, the bus," said Danny.

The bus pulled up with a roar and a hiss as the brakes released, a sound rather like the one Danny's uncle Mortimer made after Thanksgiving dinner. Danny and Wendell climbed on and sat in their usual seat.

"So . . ." said Wendell, with the air of one who already knows the answer, "did you get your science paper done?"

"Nope!" said Danny cheerfully, pulling a notebook out of his backpack. "I'm gonna do it right now."

Wendell draped himself over the back of the seat. "You've got fifteen minutes. Isn't that cutting it a little close?"

"I do my best work under pressure," said Danny. "Anyway, I've got a secret weapon."

"What's that?"

"You."

Wendell sighed. "You haven't done anything on it at all?"

Danny shrugged. "I was going to work on it this morning," he said, "but Dad wanted to give me fire-breathing lessons before he went to work."

Wendell raised an eyebrow. "And?"

"And?"

"And *how did it go?*"

Danny rubbed at the back of his neck. "Same as it ever does."

He considered telling Wendell about the morning's lecture, but decided against it. For one thing, Wendell *always* applied himself. Even in gym class, where he was completely hopeless, you couldn't say he wasn't trying. In fact, it was usually rather embarrassing just how hard he was trying.

For another thing, if he didn't hurry, he wasn't going to get his paper done.

"Never mind about the fire-breathing. Now quick, tell me everything you know about the ocean."

Wendell sighed again. For a fairly small iguana, he had an astonishing lung capacity. "It's big. It's wet. It's salty."

"That's *all* you've got?" Danny stared at him.

"It's got fish in it."

Danny groaned. "You don't know anything else about the ocean? What kind of a nerd are you?"

"I'm not a *marine* iguana. Anyway, my paper was about bats."

Danny tapped the pencil against the end of his snout. "Are there any bats that live in the ocean?"

"Not unless they wear little snorkels, no."

"Ooh, snorkels! That's perfect, Wendell." Danny began to write furiously.

The Rare and Elusive Snorkelbat!*

This wily bat left the air for the cool green depths of the ocean! When not relaxing on the beach, drinking tropical drinks with the little paper umbrellas, the snorkelbat plays in the surf, builds little sand castles, and goes diving.

*Completely a figment of Danny's imagination.

Fifteen minutes later, the bus let them out in front of the Herpitax-Phibbias School for Reptiles and Amphibians. It was a low brick building with a playground to one side, and a number of large rocks for sitting and sunning oneself.

"I still can't believe you're handing in a paper on snorkelbats," muttered Wendell.

"Worrywart," said Danny. "I bet Mr. Snaug doesn't even read these. He just grades on length."

Wendell shrugged. He'd known Danny for over a year, ever since the dragon's family had moved into the neighborhood, and he knew better than to argue.

FOOD FIGHT

The *F* was large and red and nearly blotted out Danny's name and the words *The Ocean*. Danny's eyes traveled down the page to his illustration of the snorkelbat. Mr. Snaug had written "See me after school" above it in red ink.

He looked up. Mr. Snaug, a long, whippy-tailed gecko, hung upside down from the ceiling and gave him a solemn look through glasses even thicker than Wendell's.

"Yikes," said Danny, and slid a little farther down in his chair.

"What took you so long?" asked Wendell as Danny trudged into the cafeteria, holding his tray. The iguana had draped his tail across the bench to save his friend a seat. "And what are you *eating?*"

"Mr. Snaug wants to talk to me after school," said Danny gloomily. "He didn't like my report."

"Well, you *did* make most of it up . . ." said Wendell, foolishly attempting to apply logic to the situation.

"Creativity should count!" Danny stabbed a fork into the stuff on his plate. The stuff took the fork and didn't seem to want to give it back.

"No, really . . ." said Wendell, watching Danny wrestle his fork away from the glop. "What *is* that?"

"I have no idea." Danny poked it again. "I think it may have been potato salad . . . at some point . . ."

The former potato salad took the fork away from him and made threatening gestures with it.

"Are you gonna eat that?"

"I'm trying to decide."

They stared at the potato salad some more. Wendell had brought his lunch from home, and

POTATO SALAD

A FEROCIOUS PREDATOR, WHAT THE COMMON POTATO SALAD LACKS IN BONE STRUCTURE, IT MORE THAN MAKES UP FOR IN VICIOUSNESS. A SCHOOL OF POTATO SALAD CAN SKELETONIZE A COW IN UNDER TWO WEEKS, ASSUMING THAT THE COW DOESN'T GET BORED AND MOVE.

POTATO SALAD CONTAINING CELERY CAN BE DANGEROUSLY UNPREDICTABLE AND SHOULD BE APPROACHED WITH EXTREME CAUTION.

took a bite of sandwich. The potato salad transferred its attention to what it perceived as a new threat, and shook the fork menacingly.

"I'm pretty hungry," said Danny sadly, "but I'd sort of feel bad about eating it. I mean, what if it has a family?"

"What if it has botulism?"

"What's that?"

"A kind of food poisoning. Your tongue turns all black and swells up and you die."

"Ooo! Like this?" Danny stuck his tongue out one side of his mouth and clutched at his throat, making theatrical *ack*ing sounds.

"I guess." Wendell was unimpressed.

The potato salad, however, applauded squishily.

Suddenly a shadow fell over the lunch table, accompanied by a wave of body odor that would have choked a goat.

"What's wrong, dorkbreath?" asked a nasty voice.

Danny stuffed his tongue back in his mouth and hunched his shoulders defensively. "Nothing."

There were three creatures standing over Danny and Wendell. Two of them—Jason the salamander and Harry the chameleon—were smaller than Danny, and Danny knew for a fact that Harry would turn the color of the wall, the lockers, or the floor in order to avoid a scuffle.

The owner of the voice, however, was Big Eddy. Big Eddy was a Komodo dragon, a species of giant monitor lizard. He had muscles on top of muscles, snaggled serrated teeth like a mouth full of bent steak knives, and shoulders that appeared to taper directly into his head without bothering with that whole "neck" business. He looked as if he should be slower than a turtle and dumber than a box of rocks.

The bit about the box of rocks was true, but the scary thing, the thing that made Big Eddy a really unpleasant bully, was that he was *fast*. Komodo dragons could run down deer when they wanted to.

Big Eddy generally didn't bother with deer, though. It was so much easier just to take Danny's lunch.

"You're no relative of mine," said Big Eddy. His two cronies snickered.

Danny was not particularly broken up about this, but did not think it would be diplomatic to say so.

"He's not a Komodo dragon," said Wendell unwisely. "He's a *real* dragon."

"Real dragon. Sure. If you're a real dragon, dork-breath, why can't you breathe fire?"

Danny hunched his shoulders again. "It doesn't work like that," he muttered.

It was true, though. Dragons breathed fire. It was what they did. His mother told him not to worry, that he was just a late bloomer, but that didn't do Danny much good when he *really* wanted to toast Big Eddy's toes. It was bad enough being the only dragon in a school filled with reptiles and amphibians—but to be a non-fire-breathing dragon? That was downright embarrassing.

"Go away, Eddy, you festering pustule," muttered Wendell. He had a vocabulary and wasn't afraid to use it. But he said it under his breath, just in case.

"What did you say?"

"He called you a feathery pus-tool," volunteered Jason the salamander. Jason was slimy in more ways than one. He also had excellent hearing.

"You're lucky I've got no idea what that means, nerd," growled Big Eddy. He smacked the little iguana on the back of his head. Wendell adjusted his glasses grimly.

The Komodo dragon turned his attention back to Danny and pulled back his fist. "Are you gonna give me your lunch, dorkbreath, or am I gonna have to take it?"

"Take it!" said Harry the chameleon, turning an excited shade of mottled purple.

Danny stared down at his plate. The potato salad stared fearlessly back up at him. A smile spread slowly across Danny's face. "Oh no," he said, turning back to Big Eddy. "No, you can have my lunch."

The potato salad flattened itself stealthily against the plate, fork at the ready.

"I think you'll be very happy together," said Danny.

Wendell snickered.

Big Eddy looked briefly confused, but did what he usually did when something confused him— he ignored it. He grabbed the tray from Danny's hands and stalked away, across the lunchroom.

"Want part of my sandwich?" asked Wendell.

"Sure."

They ate Wendell's sandwich in silence, waiting. After a few minutes, there was a scream from across the lunchroom. It was the exact sound that a young Komodo dragon might make when he has just been stabbed in the hand with a plastic fork by a plate of recalcitrant potato salad.

"I think we may wish to beat a strategic retreat," said Wendell. He tossed the remains of his lunch in the trash and headed for the door.

"You said it," said Danny.

THE PLAN

"So what are you going to do?" asked Wendell a few hours later as they walked toward the bus.

"About Big Eddy? I dunno. Apparently the fork didn't do much, but the potato salad bit him pretty good . . ."

"No, I mean about the *paper.* Did you talk to Mr. Snaug?"

"Yes, and he was totally unreasonable!" Danny said, flailing his arms wildly. Smoke drifted from his nostrils—he couldn't breathe fire, but he could occasionally manage a little smoke when

he was flustered. Wendell wrinkled his snout and coughed.

"Smoke . . ." he muttered.

"Right, sorry." Danny fanned the smoke away with one hand. He opened his mouth, then paused, distracted. There was a small hole under the chain-link fence around the school, where the metal links had been bent back. The tips of the chain had yellow goop on them, and there was a rather slimy yellow trail leading into the storm drain. It was almost exactly what you'd expect from the escape tunnel of a rogue potato salad making a break for freedom. Danny smiled.

Danny leaned over a bit but couldn't see anything. How long could a potato salad live in the sewers, anyway? What was the natural habitat of a potato salad?

"So what are you going to do?" asked Wendell again.

"Hmmm? Oh!" Righteous indignation reclaimed his attention. "He told me to rewrite it by tomorrow! And to actually learn something about oceans this time! Can you *believe* it?"

"He's a monster."

"Don't think that just because I'm having a crisis, I can't tell when you're being sarcastic, Wendell."

Wendell tried to look innocent. It is not a look that comes easily to iguanas. Danny punched him in the shoulder.

"So what are you going to do?" Wendell asked, rubbing his arm.

"I don't know yet. But I'll think of something before tomorrow morning."

By the time they had arrived at Danny's house, neither of them had come up with a plan. Danny had suggested hoping for a snow day. Wendell had pointed out that it was mid-April. Wendell had then suggested that Danny go to the library and actually read about oceans. This idea was met with the contempt it deserved.

The Dragonbreath house looked much like all the other houses on the block. It had nothing to suggest that the reptiles living there were semi-mythical, except for a faint clinging scent of charcoal, and a number of scorch marks on the ceiling.

"Moooooom!" Danny scooped a cookie up off the kitchen counter. "I have to write a paper about the ocean!"

His mother, who was much more a mid-afternoon person than a morning person, was no longer hunched over her coffee looking murderous. Now she was wearing a large flowered apron and humming tunelessly. She turned away from the dishes, wiping her hands on a towel, and smiled at them. "Hi, Danny. Hi, Wendell, so nice to see you. Have a cookie."

"Thank you, Mrs. Dragonbreath," said Wendell politely, and took a cookie.

"I don't know anything about the ocean," Danny complained through a spray of cookie crumbs.

"Don't talk with your mouth full, dear. Have you talked to your cousin Edward?"

"Cousin Edward's an ocean?" Danny raised a scaly eyebrow. "Why was I not informed of this?"

Wendell rolled his eyes. Danny's mother, having had a lifetime to develop an immunity to Danny's sense of humor, merely said, "No, dear, he's a sea serpent. He *lives* in the ocean—that's why he always comes here for Thanksgiving. It's so hard to cook underwater."

Danny froze, half-eaten cookie forgotten in his hand.

"Uh-oh," said Wendell, recognizing the sudden gleam in his friend's eye. He frantically looked around for something to hide behind.

"That's a great idea, Mom!"

"Oh, dear . . ." Wendell wondered if he could make it to the front door.

"We're off to sail the seven seas!"

"That's nice, dear," said his mother, turning back to the dishes. "Call if you'll be late."

"C'mon, Wendell!" said Danny, grabbing his friend's collar as he rushed for the door.

Wendell sighed. That was the trouble with being Danny's friend—you were prey to his sudden enthusiasms. The young iguana'd never really had a chance.

AHOY!

"So," said Wendell, resigned to his fate. "How are we going to find your cousin?"

"Always with the questions, Wendell. We'll take the bus."

HERE WE GO, THE SARGASSO SEA!

BUS SCHEDULE

MALL

EAST ST

SARGASSO SEA

3RD ST

LIBRARY

COMMUNITY COLLEGE

"Has it ever occurred to you to wonder why this bus goes to the Sargasso Sea?" Wendell asked as the bus chugged along. It was newer than the school bus and sounded much less like an animal was dying horribly somewhere in the engine block.

"Not really, no . . ."

In a surprisingly short time—at least, surprising to Wendell—the bus pulled up to a rickety dock. Gray, peeling wood extended out across soupy green water, webbed with weeds that looked like enormous strands of snot. Wendell shook his head in disbelief.

"Wow. For once, it actually looks like you said it would."

"Hey, mythical stuff I know . . ."

"Has this always been here?" Wendell asked the bus driver as they got off.

The bus driver, a large chameleon in a blue uniform, just flicked out a long tongue and licked it over her eyelids, snagging a fly in the process. Danny stepped off the bus.

"Of course it's always been here," he said over his shoulder. "It's the Sargasso Sea. It's been here for like forever."

"I just sorta . . . expected I would have seen it before . . ." said Wendell. He had somehow maintained a fairly solid grip on reality despite being Danny's friend, but there were limits.

"Well, you're seeing it now." Danny waited until the bus had pulled away, then hurried across the street. "C'mon. The seaweed holds stuff up. Try not to fall in, though."

The warning made sense as soon as Wendell

stepped out. The dock apparently wasn't attached to anything. Boards floated loose, in a haphazard trail out across the water. In a few places, gaps had been filled in with old barrels, crates, and a rusted Stop sign.

Danny skipped across the debris, barely paying attention to his footing. Wendell gulped and put out a hesitant foot. The board dipped under his weight. He quickly pulled his foot back. "Unnngh . . ."

"Come *on* . . ." Danny's voice floated back to him. "We don't have all week, Wendell. The paper's due tomorrow!"

Wendell gritted his teeth—he had sixty-eight of them—and stepped out onto the seaweed. He very slowly, very carefully began to tiptoe from board to board. "Eeee . . . eeee . . . *eeeee* . . ."

It took him twice as long to pick his way across the dock as it did Danny. The dragon was nearly dancing with impatience by the time Wendell finally arrived at the end of the dock.

The last stretch of dock was actually anchored to a set of pilings, and didn't move nearly so alarmingly. He resisted the urge to fall flat and kiss the boards. Danny would have never let him hear the end of it.

**DING
DONG
DING
DONG
DING
DONG
DING
DONG**

They waited. A seagull landed on the surface of the seaweed with a gloopy splash.

"Maybe he's not home," said Wendell hopefully. He wasn't entirely certain he wanted to meet a sea serpent. Danny was his best friend, and Danny's mother was awfully nice, but the iguana wasn't always sure about semi-mythical people in general. You never knew when one would turn out to eat iguanas.

"He's a *sea serpent*," said Danny. "This is the *sea*. Where else is he going to be?"

"Don't sea serpents ever— Yeerrk!"

DANNY TOLD HIS COUSIN ABOUT HIS SCIENCE
PAPER, AND HOW HE HAD TO LEARN SOMETHING
ABOUT THE OCEAN BY TOMORROW, OR GET AN F.

MINTY FRESH

"The ocean, huh?" Edward scratched his head with a flipper. "Well, I could tell you quite a lot about it . . . but it'd be a lot more interesting just to *show* you."

"You mean we could go underwater with you?" asked Danny, his eyes shining. "That would be awesome! Wouldn't it, Wendell?"

"Err," said Wendell, and then "Oof!" as Danny elbowed him in the ribs. "Um. Yeah. Awesome."

"Wait right here," said Edward, and sank back into the slimy green water.

"I really don't know about this, Danny," said Wendell as soon as the sea serpent was gone. "I mean—"

"You can swim," said Danny.

"Yeah, but I'm not a fish! I don't have gills!"

"I'm sure Cousin Edward wouldn't have suggested it if he didn't have a plan. Besides, what can possibly happen?"

Wendell thought of a half-dozen things, discarded most of them as unconvincing, and then finally said, "Sharks."

"Sharks?"

"There might be sharks."

"That would be *awesome*!"

Wendell heaved a sigh that seemed to come from the tip of his tail, and resigned himself to a watery grave.

"Here," said Edward, poking his long snout out of the water again. "Have one of these."

BREATH MINTS

NOW IN WINTERGREEN!

"Breath mints?" asked Wendell. "Do we have bad breath?" (Since Edward's breath smelled like rotten catfish, this struck him as rather presumptuous.)

"No, these are a different kind of breath mint. They give you breath for a couple of hours." Edward clapped a flipper on the small iguana's shoulder. "And they're minty fresh!"

Danny had already popped one into his mouth. Wendell followed suit. It tasted . . . fizzy. He felt as if spiders were dancing inside his lungs, wearing mint-flavored tap shoes.

"All right, then! Grab a flipper and hold on!"

The water was dark and shockingly cold. Wendell opened his mouth to yelp, and felt bubbles escaping.

Oh no! I'll drown!

Except . . . he wasn't drowning. His lungs were heaving in and out, and air was somehow pouring into them, possibly carried by the tap-dancing spiders.

"Wow!" said Danny. "These breath mints really work!" Bubbles emerged from his mouth and spiraled upward. Craning his neck, Wendell could see a dim, flickering green light overhead, where the sun filtered through the seaweed.

"They'll keep you from getting the bends too," said Edward. The sea serpent angled his head downward and began to swim with broad strokes of his tail. Wendell and Danny clung to his outstretched flippers. Water rushed past their faces like wind. The seaweed spiraled down around them like long columns of slimy ribbon.

"What are the bends?" asked Danny.

"The bends are a thing that happens to divers," said Edward, still swimming downward. "See, when you go really deep, the weight of all the water presses down on you, and you kinda squish a bit. It's okay, though, because people squish pretty well."

Wendell tried to imagine himself squishing, and turned a slightly paler shade of gray green.

"But when you swim back up again, you come unsquished," the sea serpent continued, "and people don't unsquish nearly so well. So if you come up too fast, you get little bubbles in your blood, like a can of soda."

The sea serpent leveled off and began to swim sideways, undulating like an eel. Passing fish stopped to goggle at them.

"So then if you try to come up with fizzy blood, it's like shaking a can of soda, only inside your body."

"Oooh! Neat! Do you explode?"

Wendell thought privately that Danny sounded way too excited about this prospect.

"Well, it's not quite *that* bad, but it's still awfully bad for you."

"See?" said Danny enthusiastically, twisting to look at Wendell. "We're learning something already!"

"Oh . . ." said the iguana. "Yay." An enormous fish loomed off to their left. It was nearly the size of their school bus, so Wendell was relieved to see that its mouth was nowhere near large enough to swallow an iguana or a small dragon. "So do fish ever get the bends?"

"Some of them do," said Edward. "A lot of fish live way down in the crushing deeps, and never come up at all."

Something about the phrase "crushing deeps" made Wendell's spine tingle.

"Oooh!" said Danny. "What's it like down there?"

A shrug rippled down the sea serpent's side. "Dark. Cold. Heavy. Full of some strange fish."

"Can we go there?"

"Oh *no*," moaned Wendell.

"It's really not that interesting," said Edward,

winking at Wendell. "A friend of mine is a sperm whale, and he can dive a mile and a half straight down, but whenever I go with him, there's not really much to see." He considered for a moment, his fins drifting in the current. "Of course, it might be because I'm with a gigantic predatory whale . . ."

Danny laughed. Wendell hunched down behind Edward's flipper and tried to look unappetizing.

The sea serpent cruised on through the deep green water, then started to rise toward the surface. Danny and Wendell could look down and see the sea floor beneath them. It didn't look flat and sandy, the way that Danny had always pictured—instead it was rocky and craggy, with seaweed draped over the stones like moss.

"Now this . . ." said Edward, sounding pleased, "this is much more interesting!" He pointed forward with a flipper. (Unfortunately it was the flipper that Wendell was clinging to, and the iguana squeaked as he was whipped back and forth.)

Far ahead of them, the sea floor suddenly erupted into a riot of color and motion. It looked like an underwater carnival had been set up among the stones.

"Ooooh. . . ." said Danny.

"A coral reef! Wow!" said Wendell.

"I thought you didn't know anything about the ocean," said Danny accusingly.

Wendell sniffed haughtily at him, an effect somewhat spoiled by the bubbles drifting from his nostrils.

Edward grinned. He had teeth as long as Danny's arm, the sight of which sent small creatures on the seabed diving for cover. "It's a coral reef, yes. I think you'll enjoy it. . . ."

The reef was alive with fish—great schools of tiny, brightly colored fish, big goggle-eyed loners, pairs of fish marked like tropical birds, and drab, solitary eels. Danny and Wendell hardly knew where to look first.

"The fish seem nervous about something," said Wendell. Many of the smaller fish were diving for cover whenever the three of them came near, and the bright schools were roiling and flickering in a decidedly alarmed manner.

"Sorry," said Edward sheepishly. "That's because of me." The sea serpent tried to make himself look small, which was an entirely lost cause. "Here, you guys go on . . . I'll move off a bit."

"Are you sure that's a good idea . . . ?" Wendell began, but Danny pushed past him.

"Pfff! Don't be such a worrywart, Wendell. It's not like the fish breathe fire."

By the time the iguana had thought up a really good reply to this, his friend was halfway across the reef, harassing an octopus. Wendell gave up, nervously waved to the distant Edward, and swam to join Danny.

"Look!" said the dragon excitedly. "It can change colors!"

The octopus obligingly turned purple, then

white, then purple with white stripes.

Wendell was forced to admit that this was indeed pretty cool. The octopus waved a tentacle smugly and added green polka dots.

"Bet you can't do plaid!" said Danny.

It blinked several times, then screwed up its eyes and gritted its beak. Danny and Wendell leaned forward, fascinated. Colors split and scattered across its skin.

With an almost audible *pop!* the stripes wavered, straightened, and turned into a quite respectable plaid.

Danny and Wendell cheered. The octopus flapped a tentacle at them, looking dazed, then turned a rather dull pink and crawled away under a rock.

"That was awesome!"

Wendell pawed the last of the sea cucumber's guts out of his ears. "What? You want even *weirder* fish? It wasn't enough getting nearly eaten by a shark and barfed on by a—sea—slug—thing—"

"Actually, sea slugs are something else again," said Edward helpfully. "That was a sea cucumber, which is an invertebrate—"

"I don't care!" Wendell tried to throw his hands in the air, realized too late that he was underwater, and flailed rather aimlessly instead. Danny had to grab his tail to haul him back down to the reef. "There could be all kinds of monsters down there!"

"Well, of course there could be," said Danny. "What's wrong with that?"

It occurred to Wendell that he was talking to a dragon and a sea serpent, who might well be related to whatever sort of monsters were lurking in the ocean depths.

"Besides," said Danny, slapping the iguana on the back, "it'll be an adventure! You worry too much! How long have you known me? Have I gotten you killed yet?"

"A shark nearly *ate* us ten minutes ago!"

"But it didn't, did it?"

He was doing it again, Wendell thought. Danny had this habit of sounding dreadfully reasonable, and then no matter what Wendell said, he sounded like an idiot, or worse, a wimp, and then before the iguana quite knew what was happening, he was doing something that would require firefighters, long explanations to his parents, or on one memorable occasion, sixteen stitches.

Wendell adjusted his glasses, which kept trying to float off his nose, and sighed. The bubbles from the sigh slipped around the sides of his snout and went skittering off toward the surface of the sea. Wendell wished he could follow them.

"If I get eaten," he said grimly, "I am *never* speaking to you again, Danny Dragonbreath."

"Fair enough," said Danny, grinning like a shark himself. "C'mon, Edward! Let's go see the weird fish!"

"Sure," said Edward. "There should be about an hour left on the breath mints. Grab a fin . . ."

"Atlantis is *real?*"

"Very real, and very determined to stay lost," said Edward. In the distance, tough-looking mer-folk with bristling crests patrolled the battlements. They carried spears and harpoons. Wendell could feel their hostile stares even from so far away.

"Can we—" Danny began.

"Afraid not." Edward put on an extra burst of speed.

Two burly mermen emerged from the city and began to swim toward them. Wendell tensed, and even Danny looked a bit alarmed. But after a few moments, the mermen turned back around.

"They're not going to hurt us," said Edward, "but they want to make sure we don't get any closer. As soon as somebody shows up and puts them in danger of being the *found* city of Atlantis, they throw him in the dungeon and feed him to the lobsters."

"You can feed somebody to lobsters?" asked Danny.

"You can when the lobsters are twenty feet long, sure . . ."

Wendell twitched. "They sound unfriendly," he said faintly.

"Let's just say that tourism is not one of their major industries."

ARRRR . . . TREASURE

They left the mermen behind and continued across the ocean bottom. The sea floor here was flat, sandy, and largely featureless, the way that Wendell and Danny had always pictured the bottom of the ocean.

Something loomed up on the horizon. It was much smaller than the city of Atlantis, but a lot closer. "Ooo!" said Danny, pointing and hopping excitedly (as much as one can hop when tucked behind the flipper of a swimming sea serpent). "Is that what I think it is?"

There was a definite smile in Edward's voice. "I thought you might like that. . . ."

It was a sunken ship. The mast jutted up at an angle, the yardarms broken and slimed with algae. There was a gaping hole in the side of the ship. It looked cold and lonely and long-dead.

"Ohmygodthatisthecoolestthingeverarealpirateshipcanwegoseeitcanwecanwe!?" gasped Danny on one breath. Danny's hoard consisted of a couple of bottle caps and most of a roll of quarters, all tucked into his mattress. But a whole sunken pirate ship? It was a dragon's dream come true.

"Sure," said Edward, changing direction with a flick of his tail.

"There aren't any sharks in it, are there?" asked Wendell warily.

"No, no," said Edward. "Well . . . not big ones anyway."

They swam at the opening in the side of the ship. Edward lowered his flippers and let the two boys swim forward.

Everything was slimy. What didn't have slime had barnacles and mussels and shellfish. It was no longer possible to read the name of the ship under the coating, and the dim interior of the ship looked more like the coral reef than like anything made by people.

"Was this a pirate ship?" asked Danny excitedly.

"I don't think so," said Edward. "It's too wide, and the masts—what's left of the masts—weren't tall enough. I think it was probably a merchant ship."

"Was it *sunk* by pirates?" Danny had never been one to let go of a promising idea.

"That's possible," Edward admitted. "Or a storm. It certainly didn't hit a rock in this area, anyway . . ."

Wendell put a hand on a crusted plank and watched a crab skitter away. It was hard to tell what things were, under their coating of ocean debris. Irregular shapes might have been old barrels or trunks, or merely broken boards. They could have been surrounded by chests of gold doubloons and it would have been impossible to tell.

The giant steering wheel lay off to one side, still recognizable under the slime. A broken hole in the deck showed where it had come crashing down, but it was impossible to tell if that had happened during the wreck, or some time later. One of the cannons lay on its back in the corner, barrel pointed upward. Judging from the suspiciously clean area around the muzzle opening, something was living inside the cannon, but Wendell wasn't about to go stick his snout in and find out what.

"Could there be treasure inside?" Danny asked.

"Not anymore," said Edward with the guilty air of one who knew exactly where the treasure had gone. (Sea serpents are not *quite* dragons, but they like to keep a hoard around just the same.) Danny snickered.

The small dragon swam inside the ship, followed by the nervous iguana, and as much of Edward as would fit.

"There's another room in here," said Danny,

peering down into a dark rectangle edged irregularly with mussels. Because the ship lay on its side, the doorway was nearly horizontal.

"That's the hold," said Edward. "Well . . . *was* the hold. It's where they kept the cargo."

Wendell joined him at the opening to the hold and looked down.

Wendell was just about to say something along the lines of "Well, nothing to see, then," or "Maybe we should go back," when Danny grabbed the edge of the doorway, kicked both feet and his tail, and swung into the darkened heart of the ship.

"Dude!"

"Ooo! Wendell, man, you gotta see this!"

Wendell gritted his teeth, but he couldn't very well back down. He lowered himself, rather hesitantly, into the dark.

It wasn't actually dark. The area where he and Danny swam lay in deep shadow, but a good chunk of the ship's keel had rotted away on the far side, and beams of eerie blue light streamed through. The light seemed to dance and move, like a curtain of crystal beads. It didn't look quite right—

"Look out!" said Wendell, suddenly realizing what he was seeing. "Jellyfish!"

"Jellyfish?" asked Danny. "Where?"

"Neat!" said Danny, starting forward. Wendell tackled him from behind.

"Hey!"

"They're poisonous, idiot!" snapped the iguana, who was starting to think the sea cucumber had been the least of his worries. "If you brush up against the tentacles, they sting you!"

Danny halted. "Like bees?" He wasn't fond of bees, after that one incident with the hose and the lawnmower. The people at the emergency room had been awfully sarcastic. Sure, he'd been in three times that week, but it was for three completely unrelated incidents! It could have happened to anybody!

"Like bees," said Wendell, who knew all about the incident.

"How do you know that?" asked Danny.

"How do you *not* know that?"

"You know, if you'd mentioned that when I asked you about the ocean the first time, we could've avoided this whole trip . . ."

Wendell rolled his eyes and swam upward into the main bulk of the ship. Danny came up behind him.

"Jellyfish?" said Edward when they told him. "They didn't used to be there. I'll have to keep that in mind . . ."

IT'S VERY, VERY DARK IN HERE

The sunken ship was long out of sight when the ground seemed to open up, becoming deeper and rockier. It was strange to look over the edge of the cliffs—Wendell's gut insisted that he was at a great height and about to fall. Wendell told his gut to shut up. He'd never been scared of heights. Apparently being scared of depths was something else again.

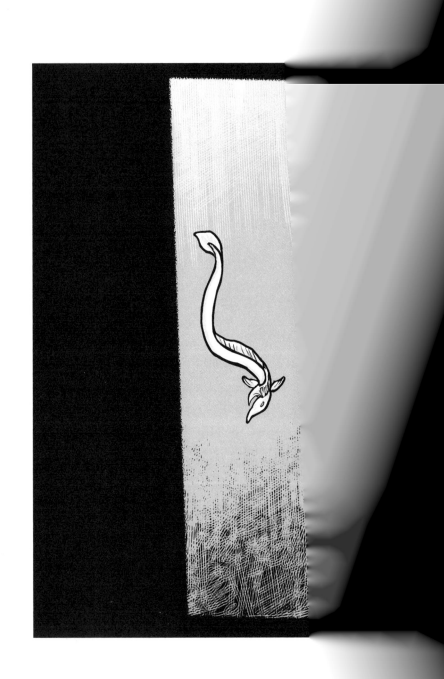

The darkness pressed in on them as the angler fish swam away. Unlike regular dark, this was thick and suffocating and alive. Even though the breath mints kept air pouring into their lungs, the two surface dwellers found themselves gasping.

Something soft and slimy brushed Wendell's tail, and he yanked it in with a yelp. Danny floated in the dark with apparent nonchalance, but Wendell was pretty sure that the bubbles floating upward in the dark were full of futile smoke.

Maybe this hadn't been such a good idea after all.

"Hang on . . ." said Edward. "I can make a light, I think . . . I'm just not sure what will happen if I do."

Wendell pressed in close against the sea serpent's scaly side. "What might happen?"

"Things down here are attracted by light," said Edward, sounding distracted. "They don't see it very often. I'm not sure who might show up . . ."

"There's so many of them!"

"They're not aggressive . . . mostly . . ." said Edward soothingly. "They're just interested in the light."

"They've got an awful lot of teeth . . ." said Wendell.

"Well, to be fair, so do we," Danny pointed out, and grinned toothily at one of the fish.

It goggled at him. So far as Danny could see, it didn't have any teeth at all, just a huge flat sucker mouth.

"What's that one?" he asked. "And that one . . . and that one over there . . . and . . . whoa! What's *that*?"

Danny felt terrible. Mostly because the giant tentacle wrapped around him was making his ribs creak with strain, but there was definitely some guilt in there too. He'd dragged his best friend off on a wild adventure, and now they were going to get hideously smooshed and eaten, possibly not in that order.

It was one thing to bring Cousin Edward along—Edward was mythological, after all, and was used to this sort of thing—but Wendell was an iguana. Epic tales of heroism and disaster were notably lacking in iguanas. His best friend just wasn't cut out for high drama.

The giant squid raised them up, one in front of each eye. Its eyes were huge and glassy, as emotionless as dinner plates. It appeared to weigh the two of them thoughtfully, then it lowered the tentacle containing Wendell. The sheaf of tentacles opened, and Danny caught a glimpse of a giant chomping beak.

It was going to eat Wendell.

Wendell screamed in the purest of pure panic.

If only I could breathe fire, Danny thought miserably. *I'd roast this big squid so fast . . .*

Smoke drifted from his nostrils as he struggled helplessly against the tentacle. It was like a band of rubbery steel. There was no escape. He and Wendell were squid food.

If only I could breathe fire!

Wendell saw the beak moving toward him, and his scream promptly climbed up the register until bats could probably hear it.

Danny took a deep, deep breath, felt the air fizzing in his lungs, and tried to concentrate on all the things his father had told him about breathing fire. He couldn't remember any of them. All he could think of was Wendell getting dragged toward that massive beak, and the fact that it was all his fault.

His lungs were burning. He was holding his breath. His sinuses felt like they were packed full of pepper.

Danny opened his mouth and felt something happening—something way down in his throat, something that felt halfway between a sneeze and a hiccup. He coughed twice—and breathed fire.

As Wendell later said, it would have been a really impressive, heroic moment . . . *if they hadn't been underwater at the time.*

As it was, though, the fire turned immediately into steam when it hit the water, scalding Danny's snout and making him squeeze his eyes shut with a yelp. Two smaller bubbles shot out of his nostrils. It was like sneezing lava.

He didn't quite roast the squid, but still, it was enough. A massive bubble of steam boiled out of Danny's mouth and smacked the squid directly in the eye.

The squid made a keening noise even higher pitched than Wendell's scream, and flailed its tentacles wildly. Dragon and iguana were thrown free.

"Help!" shouted Wendell, thinking quickly. "Edward, *help!*"

Danny would have shouted too, but the inside of his mouth felt broiled. He touched his tongue carefully to his lips and winced. It was almost exactly like when he tried to eat pizza that was too hot and scalded the roof of his mouth. Except this feeling went most of the way down his throat.

"Ow . . ." he said.

"EDWARD!" screamed Wendell, who apparently had lungs like an opera singer.

Edward made a loop out of his body and pulled the exhausted dragon and iguana under a flipper. "When I couldn't draw it off, I knew I'd need to get help. Kraken aren't very common, but they're *nasty*."

"We saw," said Wendell faintly.

"Actually, they're delicious," said the whale. It was twice the size of the giant squid. Edward looked like a garter snake next to it.

"This is my friend Eee!aee!(click)ee'ee'aiiee-(click!)*," said Edward.

"Gotta show those squid who's boss," said Eee!aee!(click)ee'ee'aiiee(click!). Its hide was mottled gray green in the dim light, and patches with barnacles like scales. One stroke of its immense tail sent such a ripple through the water that Wendell and Danny had to cling tightly to Edward's flipper to avoid being carried off by the wave.

*That's whale for "Eats-a-lot-of-squid."

129

THANK YOU, MR. WHALE!
YOU GOT HERE JUST IN TIME! I THOUGHT WE WERE GONERS!

GLAD I COULD HELP.
I BETTER GO MAKE SURE IT'S REALLY GONE.

LAND, HO!

It took a surprisingly short time to reach the surface again, but it couldn't be soon enough for Wendell. The iguana climbed out on the dock, assisted with a bump by Edward, and flattened himself on the boards with a noise that wasn't quite a whimper.

Danny nobly decided not to notice his friend's display and turned back to his cousin. "Thanks for everything, Edward! That was great!"

"I'm glad you enjoyed it," said Edward, dipping his fins.

SMOOCH SMOOCH SMOOCH SMOOCH SMOOCH SMOOCH

A noise came from Wendell that sounded vaguely like "muttermutter*shark*grumblemutter-*giantsquid*—"

Edward looked at Danny. Danny looked at Edward. They both looked at Wendell. They looked back at each other. They shrugged.

"C'mon, Wendell," said Danny, heaving a sigh. "Let's get you home before you melt like a little tadpole."

"I am not melting," said Wendell with great dignity. "I am freaking out. There is a difference."

"If you say so," said Danny, letting out a long smoky sigh. He got an arm under Wendell's shoulders and hauled him upright.

By the time the bus rumbled into view, Wendell had regained his composure and was pretending that he had not just been clinging to the dock as if it were a security blanket. And he *definitely* hadn't fallen down and kissed the sidewalk. Absolutely not. Anybody who said differently was asking for trouble.

Danny didn't bring up the ground-kissing, at least for the moment. After all, he still felt terrible about getting his friend tangled up in a giant squid tentacle. (The next time Danny needed to blackmail the iguana for something, mind you, he had some excellent material. He'd be working on his imitation of Wendell kissing the sidewalk for a long time to come.)

"So," said the iguana, hanging over the back of

one of the seats. "You think you got enough material for your paper now? Because if not—"

"Oh, relax," said Danny. "Are you kidding? I could write two papers! Maybe three." He frowned. "Possibly four, but I'd have to include some of the unbelievable stuff . . ."

"'How I Nearly Became Fish Food,' by Danny Dragonbreath," said Wendell snidely.

"I may leave that bit out." Danny frowned down at his claws. "Mr. Snaug would never believe it anyway."

"Just as long as we don't have to do this again . . ."

"Don't worry. I'll write it up tomorrow morning, it'll be fine . . ."

Wendell's glare could have melted concrete.

"Oh, come on, it's not like the squid *actually* ate you . . ."

Wendell's glare intensified. Diamonds would have gone soft and runny under that glare.

Danny heaved a sigh and puffed out a little bit of smoke. "Fine, fine . . . I'll do it tonight . . ."

"Dad!" said Danny, coming down the stairs the next morning. "Dad, I did it! I breathed fire! Only once, but I did it!"

"That's my boy!" said Mr. Dragonbreath.

Mrs. Dragonbreath opened one eye and said, "Yay. Fire. Woo," then fell back asleep at the table. For her at this hour, this reaction was the equivalent of throwing confetti and bringing in a marching band. Danny beamed.

"Here you go, champ. Try it again." His dad brandished a slice of bacon on a fork.

Danny inhaled. Something between a sneeze and a hiccup . . . something right down at the bottom of his throat . . .

The resulting belch made the bacon flap gently and rattled the kitchen window, but did not produce any flames.

"That's not *quite* it," said Mr. Dragonbreath patiently. "Try it again. Think hot thoughts."

Danny screwed up his snout in concentration. He hadn't been thinking hot thoughts yesterday.

He'd been terrified out of his mind, seeing the tentacle wrap around Wendell, and hearing the iguana shrieking. He tried to remember just how scared he'd been.

Something happened in the vicinity of his stomach. Danny tried to exhale, choked, and burst into a smoky coughing fit.

"Well, you've definitely got something happening down there," said his father, pounding him on the back. "Just can't quite get to it yet. But I'm sure if you apply yourself . . ."

Danny stopped coughing long enough to sigh.

He tried breathing fire several times on the way to the bus stop, but all he managed was the smoke-filled cough. Still, it was better than nothing. He'd done it once. Surely he'd be able to do it again . . . eventually.

BULLY UP

"So he liked the paper, then," said Wendell. "Good." He surveyed the *A* with grim satisfaction. "Because I'm never, ever going back to the Sargasso Sea . . . or going with you anywhere other than the library for research."

"Oh, come on." Danny tucked the paper under his lunch tray as they walked to a bench. "You gotta admit, there were some fun bits. Remember when that sea cucumber was all . . . bleh . . . and—"

"I don't have to admit *anything*."

Danny might have continued the argument, but a vast form loomed up in front of them. And the form had one hand wrapped up in a bandage.

Big Eddy was not pleased.

His two henchmen, the salamander and the chameleon, were lurking behind him. Harry was turning blue and green with excitement, and Jason kept rubbing his webbed fingers together.

"Your stupid lunch bit me, dorkbreath," he growled at Danny.

Danny opened his mouth to say something, but Wendell beat him to it. "His *lunch* bit you?" said the iguana, voice dripping with scorn. "Do you know how crazy that sounds?"

There was a brief pause.

Looking as if he wished he were somewhere else, Jason rubbed the back of his neck and said, "That, um, does sound a little odd, boss."

Apparently now that he'd said it out loud, Big Eddy *did* realize how crazy it sounded. He flushed a little pink around the scales and shuffled heavily clawed feet.

"What did it do, sink little potato-y fangs into you?" said Danny.

"Are you sure there wasn't something in it? Like a thumbtack, maybe?" asked Harry, and then promptly turned the color of the floor.

The Komodo dragon flushed harder, but rallied himself, lashing his thick tail. "Doesn't matter," Big Eddy said. "Give me your lunch."

"So you say his lunch bit you," said Wendell, who was apparently feeling particularly suicidal today, "and now you want to take his lunch *again*? Talk about not learning from your mistakes . . ."

Big Eddy blinked a few times and ran a finger nervously over his bandage.

"You sure you want it?" asked Danny. "It's looking particularly vicious today. . . ." He clutched the edges of the tray as if trying to contain it. (Actually, today's slice of cheese pizza was completely docile, though the green beans did look as

if they might be plotting something.)

Big Eddy actually took a step backward.

There was a quickly stifled snigger from one of his henchmen. The Komodo dragon wheeled around and glared. Even though both the salamander and the chameleon had completely blank faces, the underside of Harry's tail was suspiciously orange with amusement.

"He's no giant squid," said Danny sadly.

"Not even a reef shark," agreed Wendell.

They carefully stepped around the baffled bully and made their way to the table.

"How long do you think that'll hold him?" asked Danny, taking a big bite of cheese pizza, which thankfully did not bite back. He wondered briefly how the potato salad was doing, out there in the storm sewers.

"I give it three days, tops," said Wendell, biting into his own completely dormant sandwich.

"Still, three days is three days . . ."

"Yup."

THAT NIGHT . . .

PSSST! HEY! TURN THE PAGE FOR MORE!

URSULA VERNON (www.ursulavernon.com) has written and illustrated one other middle-grade novel: *Nurk: The Strange, Surprising Adventures of a (Somewhat) Brave Shrew*. The daughter of an artist, she attempted to rebel and become a scientist, but in the end couldn't fight her destiny. She lives in Pittsboro, NC, where she writes, draws, and creates oddities.